LOOKING FOR A KING

An Anthology for Christmas

Ronald Whetton

LOOKING FOR A KING

An Anthology for Christmas

London SPCK

First published 1978
SPCK
Holy Trinity Church
Marylebone Road
London NW1 4DU

Printed in Great Britain by
Bocardo & Church Army Press Ltd
Cowley, Oxford

ISBN 0 281 03621 7

For the three Rs

Rennie, Rachel, and Robert

With love from the Fourth

CONTENTS

PREFACE

This little book on the theme of Christmas is based on a collection of material I began as a boy. So much has been written on the subject that it is impossible for compiler or publisher to be definitive or comprehensive about it and, for various reasons, some material has had to be excluded from this volume. There is, of course, much I have yet to discover. So, my apologies should you not find your favourite carol, poem or story herein. Generally, I have tried not to include material which can readily be found in, for example, *The Oxford Book of Carols* and Church hymnals, though there are included a few carols with sentiments which appealed to me as a boy in Sunday School and, obviously, still do.

Those of you in churches or schools who are looking for material on the Christmas theme may find this book useful, and all who acknowledge and celebrate Christmas, in its 'bits and pieces'—both old and new, find once again God's promise renewed and fulfilled in the coming of the Christ child.

RONALD WHETTON

January 1978

Prophecy

PREPARE YE THE WAY OF THE LORD

Comfort ye, comfort ye my people, saith your God.

Speak ye comfortably to Jerusalem, and cry unto her, that her warfare is accomplished, that her iniquity is pardoned; for she hath received of the Lord's hand double for all her sins.

The voice of him that crieth in the wilderness, Prepare ye the way of the Lord, make straight in the desert a highway for our God.

Every valley shall be exalted, and every mountain and hill shall be made low; and the crooked shall be made straight, and the rough places plain;

And the glory of the Lord shall be revealed, and all flesh shall see it together; for the mouth of the Lord hath spoken it.

The voice said, Cry. And he said, What shall I cry? All flesh is grass, and all the goodliness thereof is as the flower of the field;

The grass withereth, the flower fadeth; because the spirit of the Lord bloweth upon it: surely the people is grass.

The grass withereth, the flower fadeth; but the word of our God shall stand for ever.

O Zion, that bringest good tidings, get thee up into the high mountain; O Jerusalem, that bringest good tidings, lift up thy voice with strength; lift it up, be not afraid; say unto the cities of Judah, Behold your God!

Behold, the Lord God will come with strong hand, and his arm shall rule for him; behold, his reward is with him, and his work before him.

He shall feed his flock like a shepherd; he shall gather the lambs with his arm, and carry them in his bosom, and shall gently lead those that are with young.

Isaiah

THE WORD TO BE MADE FLESH

There appeared a man named John, sent from God; he came as a witness to testify to the light, that all might become believers through him. He was not himself the light; he came to bear witness to the light. The real light which enlightens every man was even then coming into the world.

He was in the world; but the world, though it owed its being to him, did not recognise him. He entered his own realm, and his own would not receive him. But to all who did receive him, to those who have yielded him their allegiance, he gave the right to become children of God, not born of any human stock, or by the fleshly desire of a human father, but the offspring of God himself. So the Word became flesh; he came to dwell among us, and we saw his glory, such glory as befits the Father's only Son, full of grace and truth.

St John

A MOMENT IN TIME

Then came, at a predetermined moment, a moment in time and of time. A moment not out of time, but in time, in what we call history; transecting, bisecting the world of time, a moment in time but not like a moment of time.
A moment in time but time was made through that moment: for without the meaning there is no time, and that moment of time gave the meaning.
Then it seemed as if men must proceed from light to light, in the light of the Word,
Through the Passion and Sacrifice saved in spite of their negative being;
Bestial as always before, carnal, self-seeking as always before, selfish and purblind as ever before,
Yet always struggling, always reaffirming, always resuming their march on the way that was lit by the light;
Often halting, loitering, straying, delaying, returning, yet following no other way.

T. S. Eliot

THE ANNUNCIATION

In the sixth month the angel Gabriel was sent from God to a town in Galilee called Nazareth, with a message for a girl betrothed to a man named Joseph, a descendant of David; the girl's name was Mary. The angel went in and said to her, 'Greetings, most favoured one! The Lord is with you.' But she was deeply troubled by what he said and wondered what this greeting might mean. Then the angel said to her, 'Do not be afraid, Mary, for God has been gracious to you; you shall conceive and bear a son, and you shall give him the name Jesus. He will be great; he will bear the title "Son of the Most High"; the Lord God will give him the throne of his ancestor David, and he will be king over Israel for ever; his reign shall never end.' 'How can this be,' said Mary, 'when I have no husband?' The angel answered, 'The Holy Spirit will come upon you; and the power of the Most High will overshadow you; and for that reason the holy child to be born will be called "Son of God"...' 'Here am I,' said Mary; 'I am the Lord's servant; as you have spoken, so be it.'

St Luke

THE CHERRY-TREE CAROL

Joseph was an old man,
An old man was he
When he wedded Mary
In the land of Galilee.

Joseph and Mary walking
In the midst of a wood
Saw berries and cherries
As red as the blood.

O then bespoke Mary,
So meek and so mild
'Pray get me one cherry,
For I am with child.'

O then bespoke Joseph,
So rude and unkind,
'Let him get thee a cherry
That got thee with child.'

O then bespoke the babe
Within his mother's womb,
'Bow down, thou tall cherry-tree,
And give my mother some.'

Then bowed down the tall cherry-tree
To his mother's right hand,
And she cried, 'See, Joseph,
I have cherries at command!'

And Mary ate her cherry
As red as the blood;
Then Mary went on
With her heavy load.

An old ballad

AS JOSEPH WAS A-WALKIN'

As Joseph was a-walkin',
He heard an angel sing,
'This night shall be the birth-night
Of Christ our Heavenly King.

'His birth-bed shall be neither
In house nor in hall,
Nor in the place of paradise
But in the oxen's stall.

'He neither shall be rocked
In silver nor in gold,
But in the wooden manger
That lieth in the mould.

'He neither shall be washen
With white wine nor with red,
But with the fair spring water
That on you shall be shed.

'He neither shall be clothed
In purple nor in pall,
But in the fair, white linen
That usen babies all.'

As Joseph was a-walkin',
Thus did the angel sing,
And Mary's son at midnight
Was born to be our king.

Anonymous

A Winter Birth

IN THE BLEAK MID-WINTER

In the bleak mid-winter
   Frosty wind made moan,
Earth stood hard as iron,
   Water like a stone;
Snow had fallen, snow on snow,
   Snow on snow,
In the bleak mid-winter
   Long ago.

Our God, heaven cannot hold Him,
   Nor earth sustain;
Heaven and earth shall flee away
   When He comes to reign:
In the bleak mid-winter
   A stable-place sufficed
The Lord God Almighty
   Jesus Christ.

Enough for Him, whom cherubim
   Worship night and day,
A breastful of milk
   And a mangerful of hay;
Enough for Him, whom angels
   Fall down before,
The ox and ass and camel
   Which adore.

Angels and archangels
   May have gathered there,
Cherubim and seraphim
   Thronged the air;

But only His mother
   In her maiden bliss
Worshipped the Beloved
   With a kiss.

Christina Georgina Rossetti

A CHRISTMAS CAROL

Before the paling of the stars,
  Before the winter morn,
Before the earliest cock-crow,
  Jesus Christ was born;
Born in a stable,
  Cradled in a manger,
In the world His Hands had made
  Born a stranger.

Priest and King lay fast asleep
  In Jerusalem,
Young and old lay fast asleep
  In crowded Bethlehem;
Saint and angel, ox and ass,
  Kept a watch together
Before the Christmas daybreak
  In the winter weather.

Jesus on His mother's breast
  In the stable cold,
Spotless Lamb of God was He,
  Shepherd of the Fold:
Let us kneel with Mary Maid,
  With Joseph bent and hoary,
With saint and angel, ox and ass,
  To hail the King of Glory.

Christina Georgina Rossetti

NEW PRINCE, NEW POMP

Behold a silly tender Babe,
  In freezing winter night,
In homely manger trembling lies;
  Alas, a piteous sight!

The inns are full, no man will yield
  This little pilgrim bed;
But forced he is with silly beasts
  In crib to shroud his head.

Despise him not for lying there:
  First what he is inquire.
An orient pearl is often found
  In depth of dirty mire.

Weigh not his crib, his wooden dish,
  Nor beasts that by him feed;
Weigh not his mother's poor attire,
  Nor Joseph's simple weed.

This stable is a prince's court;
  The crib, his chair of state;
The beasts are parcel of his pomp;
  The wooden dish his plate.

The persons in that poor attire
  His royal liveries wear.
The Prince himself is come from heaven;
  This pomp is praisèd there.

With joy approach, O Christian wight!
  Do homage to thy King;
And highly praise this humble pomp
  Which he from heaven doth bring.

Robert Southwell

A CHRISTMAS CAROL

When from His throne the Godhead bowed
To human Form below
The Heavens dropt down, and every cloud
Hung loath to let Him go.
Oh bright the light and white the night,
When full of favour stored,
God's Maid lay down in Bethlehem town,
To wait the coming Lord!

Before His Feet went down the snow
Amid the tranquil night,
Till all the world lay white below
To greet the Lord of Light,
Oh bright the light and white the night,
When full of favour stored,
God's Maid lay down in Bethlehem town,
To wait the coming Lord!

The rugged hills and all the rocks
Were covered as with fleece;
The towns were seen like folded flocks
To wait the Prince of Peace.
Oh bright the light and white the night,
When full of favour stored,
God's Maid lay down in Bethlehem town,
To wait the coming Lord!

Oh, like a flock in field and fold,
The wintry world lay then,
On that fair night in days of old
When Christ came down to men,

Oh bright the light and white the night,
When full of favour stored,
God's Maid lay down in Bethlehem town,
To wait the coming Lord!

Laurence Housman

A COUNTRY CAROL

Deep in the woods the foxes bark,
And skinned of cloud the moon rides high.
In meadows where the summer lark
Untwists her song, snow-banks lie.
  The faithful say
  This winter night is articled,
  Auspicious for the burning child.

A country coming is foretold
As usual. Stall, ox, and ass
Are ready. Someone has lit the lamps and boiled
Water. Straw bales gleam like brass.
  The faithful pray
  Let God and man be reconciled,
  And keep the bargain of the burning child.

Their prayers swarm up as glib as mottoes,
Leaving behind them other members of the feast:
Broilers penned in twilight ghettos,
Shackled calves, and rabbits dying of pest.
  The burning child descends,
  A mirror for our charity.
  This time, for us to burn; for us to die.

Philip Oakes

THE SHEEP ON BLACKENING FIELDS

The sheep on blackening fields
No weather-warning know
As the thin, sapping sun
Annihilates the snow.
Winter has eased its grip,
The struck fountain flows;
Burns in its lamp of leaves
The white flame of the rose.

In the stiff river's gut
Fish and blurred stars unfreeze;
Unclench at the moor's side
The fists of trees.
Unscientifically housed
And in his hand a stone,
Grizzles in dusty hay
A naked child, alone.

A star of bitter red
Above the mountain crest
Writes on the squalling dark,
Christus natus est.
Silently we renew
The spoiled bread, the burned wine;
Take the huge-bellied child
Whose flesh is yours, is mine.

Charles Causley

SONG FOR A WINTER BIRTH

Under the watchful lights
   A child was born;
From a mortal house of flesh
   Painfully torn.

And we, who later assembled
   To praise or peer,
Saw merely an infant boy
   Soft sleeping there;

Till he awoke and stretched
   Small arms wide
And, for food or comfort,
   Quavering cried,

A cry and attitude
   Rehearsing, in small,
The deathless death still haunting
   The Place of the Skull.

Outside, in the festive air,
   We lit cigars;
The night was nailed to the sky
   With hard bright stars.

Vernon Scannell

The Shepherds

THE BIRTH AND ITS TELLING TO THE SHEPHERDS

In those days a decree was issued by the Emperor Augustus for a general registration throughout the Roman world. This was the first registration of its kind; it took place when Quirinius was governor of Syria. For this purpose everyone made his way to his own town; and so Joseph went up to Judaea from the town of Nazareth in Galilee, to be registered at the city of David, called Bethlehem, because he was of the house of David by descent; and with him went Mary who was betrothed to him. She was pregnant, and while they were there the time came for her child to be born, and she gave birth to a son, her first-born. She wrapped him round, and laid him in a manger, because there was no room for them to lodge in the house.

Now in this same district there were shepherds out in the fields, keeping watch through the night over their flock, when suddenly there stood before them an angel of the Lord, and the splendour of the Lord shone round them. They were terror-struck, but the angel said, 'Do not be afraid; I have good news for you: there is great joy coming to the whole people. Today in the city of David a deliverer has been born to you—the Messiah, the Lord. And this is your sign: you will find a baby lying all wrapped up, in a manger.' All at once there was with the angel a great company of the heavenly host, singing the praises of God:

'Glory to God in highest heaven,
And on earth his peace for men on whom his favour rests.'

After the angels had left them and gone into heaven the shepherds said to one another, 'Come, we must go straight to Bethlehem and see this thing that has happened, which the Lord has made known to us.' So they went with all speed and found their way to Mary and Joseph; and the baby was lying in the manger. When they saw him, they recounted what they had been told about this child; and all who heard were astonished at what the shepherds said. But Mary treasured up all these things and pondered over them. Meanwhile the shepherds returned glorifying and praising God for what they had heard and seen; it had all happened as they had been told.

St Luke

SHEPHERD'S SONG

As I rode out this enderes* night,
Of three jolly shepherds I saw a sight,
And all about their fold a star shone bright;
They sang, Terli, terlow;
So merrily the shepherds their pipes can blow.

Down from heaven, from heaven so high,
Of angels there came a great company.
With mirth, and joy, and great solemnity
They sang, Terli, terlow;
So merrily the shepherds their pipes can blow.

Anonymous

*enderes—last

THE SHEPHERDS' CAROL

We stood on the hills, Lady,
Our day's work done,
Watching the frosted meadows
That winter had won.

The evening was calm, Lady,
The air so still,
Silence more lovely than music
Folded the hill.

There was a star, Lady,
Shone in the night,
Larger than Venus it was
And bright, so bright.

Oh, a voice from the sky, Lady,
It seemed to us then
Telling of God being born
In the world of men.

And so we have come, Lady,
Our day's work done,
Our love, our hopes, ourselves
We give to your son.

Anonymous

Mother and Child

A CRADLE HYMN

Hush! my dear, lie still and slumber;
  Holy angels guard thy bed!
Heavenly blessings without number
  Gently falling on thy head.

How much better thou'rt attended
  Than the Son of God could be,
When from heaven He descended
  And became a child like thee!

Soft and easy is thy cradle;
  Coarse and hard thy Saviour lay,
When His birthplace was a stable
  And His softest bed was hay.

See the kindly shepherds round Him,
  Telling wonders from the sky!
Where they sought Him, there they found Him,
  With His Virgin Mother by.

See the lovely babe a-dressing;
  Lovely infant, how He smiled!
When He wept, the mother's blessing
  Soothed and hushed the holy child.

Lo, He slumbers in His manger,
  Where the hornèd oxen fed:
Peace, my darling; here's no danger,
  Here's no ox anear thy bed.

Isaac Watts

A CHRISTMAS CAROL

The Christ-child lay on Mary's lap,
His hair was like a light.
(O weary, weary were the world,
But here is all aright.)

The Christ-child lay on Mary's breast
His hair was like a star.
(O stern and cunning are the Kings,
But here the true hearts are.)

The Christ-child lay on Mary's heart,
His hair was like a fire.
(O weary, weary is the world,
But here the world's desire.)

The Christ-child stood at Mary's knee,
His hair was like a crown,
And all the flowers looked up at Him,
And all the stars looked down.

G. K. Chesterton

MOTHER AND MAIDEN

I sing of a maiden
  That is matchless.
King of all kings
  For her son she chose.

He came all so still
  Where his mother was,
As dew in April
  That falleth on the grass.

He came all so still,
  To his mother's bower,
As dew in April
  That falleth on the flower.

He came all so still—
  There his mother lay,
As dew in April
  That falleth on the spray.

Mother and maiden
  Was never none but she;
Well may such a lady
  God's mother be.

A fifteenth-century carol

A ROCKING HYMN

Sweet baby, sleep; what ails my dear?
What ails my darling thus to cry?
Be still, my child, and lend thine ear
To hear me sing thy lullaby:
My pretty lamb, forbear to weep;
Be still, my dear; sweet baby, sleep.

Thou blessèd soul, what canst thou fear?
What thing to thee can mischief do?
Thy God is now thy father dear;
His holy spouse thy mother too.
Sweet baby, then forbear to weep;
Be still, my babe; sweet baby, sleep.

While thus thy lullaby I sing
For thee great blessings ripening be:
Thine oldest Brother is a King,
And hath a kingdom bought for thee.
Sweet baby, then forbear to weep;
Be still, my babe; sweet baby, sleep.

Sweet baby, sleep, and nothing fear;
For whosoever thee offends
By thy Protector threatened are,
And God and angels are thy friends.
Sweet baby, then forbear to weep;
Be still, my babe; sweet baby, sleep.

When God with us was dwelling here,
In little babes He took delight,
Such innocents as thou, my dear,
Are ever precious in His sight.
Sweet baby, then forbear to weep;
Be still, my babe; sweet baby, sleep.

A little infant once was He,
And strength in weakness then was laid
Upon His Virgin Mother's knee,
That power to thee might be conveyed.
Sweet baby, then forbear to weep;
Be still, my babe; sweet baby, sleep.

In this thy frailty and thy need,
He friends and helpers doth prepare,
Which thee shall cherish, clothe, and feed,
For of thy weal they tender are.
Sweet baby, then forbear to weep;
Be still, my babe; sweet baby, sleep.

The King of Kings, when He was born,
Had not so much for outward ease;
By Him such dressings were not worn,
Nor such like swaddling-clothes as these.
Sweet baby, then forbear to weep;
Be still, my babe; sweet baby, sleep.

Within a manger lodged thy Lord,
Where oxen lay, and asses fed;
Warm rooms we do to thee afford,
An easy cradle or a bed.
Sweet baby, then forbear to weep;
Be still, my babe; sweet baby, sleep.

Thou hast, yet more to perfect this,
A promise, and an earnest got
Of gaining everlasting bliss,
Though thou, my babe, perceiv'st it not.
Sweet baby, then forbear to weep;
Be still, my babe; sweet baby, sleep.

George Wither

Carol Singers

CAROL SINGERS

'Now mind neighbours,' said Old William, as they went out one by one at the door, he himself holding it ajar and regarding them with a critical face as they passed, like a shepherd counting his sheep. 'You two counterboys, keep your ears open to Michael's fingering, and don't ye go straying into the treble part along o' Dick and his set, as ye did last year; and mind this especially when we be in the "Arise, and hail". Billy Chimlen, don't you sing quite so raving mad as you fain would; and all o' ye, whatever ye do, keep from making a great scuffle on the ground when we go in at people's gates; but go quietly, so as to strike up all of a sudden, like spirits.'

'Farmer Ledlow's first?'

'Farmer Ledlow's first; the rest as usual.'

Just before the clock struck twelve they lighted the lanterns and started. The moon, in her third quarter, had risen since the snowstorm; but the dense accumulation of snow-cloud weakened her power to a faint twilight, which was rather pervasive of the landscape than traceable to the sky. The breeze had gone down, and the rustle of their feet and tones of their speech echoed with an alert rebound from every post, boundary-stone, and ancient wall they passed, even where the distance of the echo's origin was less than a few yards. . . .

They crossed to a gate in the direction of the school, which, standing on a slight eminence at the junction of the three ways, now rose in unvarying and dark flatness against the sky. . . . The band entered the school enclosure, enjoined by old William to keep upon the grass. 'Number seventy-eight,' he softly gave out as they formed round in a semicircle, the boys opening the lanterns to get a clearer light, and directing their rays on the books.

Then passed into the quiet night an ancient and time-worn hymn, embodying a quaint Christianity in words orally transmitted from father to son through several generations down to the present characters, who sang them out right earnestly.

In Bethlehem He was born
  O thou Man:
In Bethlehem He was born
  For mankind's sake.
In Bethlehem He was born,
  Christmas-day i' the morn;
Our Saviour thought no scorn
  Our faults to take.

Having concluded the last note, they listened for a minute or two but found that no sound issued from the school house.

'Four breaths, and then "O, what unbounded goodness!" number fifty-nine,' said William.

This was duly gone through, and no notice whatever seemed to be taken of the performance.

'Good guide us, surely 'tisn't a' empty house as befell us in the year thirty-nine and forty-three!' said old Dewey.

'Four breaths and then the last,' said the leader authoritatively, "Rejoice ye Tenants of the earth", number sixty-four.'

At the close, waiting yet another minute, he said in a clear loud voice, as he had said in that village at that hour and season for the previous forty years—

'A merry Christmas to ye!'

Thomas Hardy

A Child's Christmas

THROUGH A CHILD'S EYES

Winifred and Grace, aged four and six-and-a-half, lay awake on Christmas Eve gazing through the square uncurtained window at the frosty constellations of winter stars. The maids clattering in the pantry below them had at last become silent; only the occasional clank of an iron-shod hoof in the horse-pasture broke the stillness of the night—when suddenly came the crunch of feet on the gravel of the drive, the soft flicker of the lantern, and the joyous tumult of a Christmas carol. In a second the two small girls were out of bed, scampering barefoot along the nursery passage, up two steps into a terrifying stretch of unlighted corridor, past the silver cupboard that harboured ghosts and tigers, on to the front landing, and through a door into the best spare bedroom.

Peering between the slats of the venetian blind, they saw the singers with pale faces and long black coats, standing in the moonlight and starlight and lanternlight and lamplight streaming from the drawing-room window on the semi-circular sweep of the gravel. The chill draught blowing through the cold bedroom was sharp as icy water on the children's shivering bodies; they gathered their nightdresses round them and huddled ecstatically together for warmth as the twenty men and boys from the church choir went on singing round the schoolmaster's lantern. 'I can close my eyes and see them,' Winifred Holtby wrote a quarter of a century later. 'I can shut my ears and hear them; in the warmth of my lighted room I can feel the wind on my bare arms, and the chill boards under my naked feet. I can even smell the queer, cold, frosty smell of the unused bedroom. It is all there.

'But it is all mine. Nobody else can ever hear it as I heard and hear it . . . . When I die, nobody will ever again know that particular sweet, fierce exaltation which stirred the rapturous, unblurred imagination of a child.'

Vera Brittain

A VILLAGE CHRISTMAS IN BOHEMIA

Our Church celebrates various holidays which affect the heart deeply. One can scarcely imagine anything more charming than Whitsuntide or anything more earnest and sacred than Easter. The sad and melancholy character of Holy Week, followed by the solemnity of Easter Sunday, accompanies us through life. One of the most beautiful holidays is celebrated by the Church almost in the middle of winter, when the nights are virtually longest and days shortest, when the sun shines most obliquely on our fields and snow covers them all—the feast of Christmas. In many countries the day preceding the birthday celebration of our Lord is called Christmas Eve; we call it Holy Eve; the day following, Holy Day; and the night that falls between them, the Night of Consecration. The Catholic Church celebrates Christmas day, the day on which our Saviour was born, with the very greatest ecclesiastical solemnity. In most regions the hour of our Lord's birth is sanctified from midnight on with a splendid nocturnal celebration, to which the church bells invite us through the silent, dark, wintry midnight air. The residents hasten to church with lanterns, or on dark, familiar paths from the snow-covered mountains, past frost-covered forests and through creaking orchards, to the church from which the solemn tones come and which, with its high, lighted windows, stands out in the midst of the village shrouded by ice-covered trees.

The church holiday is tied up with a domestic one. In almost all Christian countries the custom has spread of showing children the arrival of the Christ child—He too was a child, the most wonderful that ever was on earth—as a happy, splendid, solemn thing, which continues to affect us throughout our whole lives; and sometimes, even in our old age, in the midst of troubled, melancholy or touching memories, it flies on bright, glittering wings through the desolate, sad and empty night sky like a backward glance into a time now past. It is customary to give children the gifts that the holy Christ child has brought, to give them happiness. This is usually done on Christmas Eve, when deep twilight has settled. Lights are lit—usually a great many—which often sway beside the little candles on the beautiful green branches of a fir or spruce tree that stands in the middle of the living room. The children are not permitted to come until the sign is given that the Holy Christ has been there and has left behind the gifts which He has brought. Then the door is opened, the little ones are permitted to enter, and in the splendid, glittering glow of the lights they see things hanging on the tree or spread out on the table which far surpass all the conceptions of their imagination, which they do not dare to touch, and which they finally, when they have been presented to them, carry about in their little arms all evening and take to bed with them. Sometimes they hear in their dreams the tones of the midnight bells which call the grown-ups to worship in church; then they imagine that the little angels are now moving through the heaven or the Holy Christ is returning home after visiting all children and leaving each of them a splendid gift.

When the following day comes, Christmas day, it is a most solemn occasion for them. In the early morning they stand in the warm living room, dressed in their best clothes; while father and mother are dressing for church. At noon they eat a formal meal, a better one than on any other day in the year. In the afternoon or towards evening friends and acquaintances come, sit about on chairs and benches and can talk to each other or comfortably look through the windows at the wintry countryside without, where either slow snowflakes are falling, or a darkening mist clings to the mountains, or the blood-red, cold sun is setting. Last night's magic presents, by now better known and more familiar, lie about in various parts of the living room, on a chair or on the bench or on the window sill.

Then the long winter passes, spring comes and the endless summer. When mother tells them again of the Holy Christ, that His holiday is coming soon and that He will come down this time too, the children feel that an eternity has passed since His last appearance and that the joy of that times lies in the far, foggy gray distance.

Because this holiday has such a lasting effect, because its reflected light reaches so far into our old age, we like to be present when children celebrate it and rejoice in it.

*Adalbert Stifter**

*Adalbert Stifter was born of peasant and artisan stock in a village in the Bohemian Forest.

A CHILD'S CHRISTMAS PRAYER

Saviour, who wast once a child
Pure and holy, undefiled,
Christmas gifts to Thee we bring
For the birthday of our King.

Innocence and happy love,
Simple trust in God above,
Youth, and hope, and joy, we lay
At Thy feet this Christmas Day.

Thou a little babe wast born
Long ago on Christmas morn;
And we would, for Thy dear sake,
More like Thine our childhood make.

Always gentle, brave, and true,
Kindly actions may we do;
In Thy footsteps we would tread,
Sunshine all around us shed.

Jesus, hear our Christmas prayer,
Keep us in Thy tender care;
And, when older grown, may we
Still Thy loving children be!

Mary Farrah

Christmas Tree

TO A YOUNG WRETCH

As gay for you to take your father's axe
As take his gun—rod—to go hunting—fishing.
You nick my spruce until its fibre cracks,
It gives up standing straight and goes down swishing.
You link an arm in its arm and you lean
Across the light snow homeward smelling green.

I could have bought you just as good a tree
To frizzle resin in a candle flame,
And what a saving 'twould have meant to me.
But tree by charity is not the same
As tree by enterprise and expedition.
I must not spoil your Christmas with contrition.

It is your Christmasses against my woods.
But even where thus opposing interests kill,
They are to be thought of as opposing goods
Oftener than as conflicting good and ill;
Which makes the war god seem no special dunce
For always fighting on both sides at once.

And though in tinsel chain and popcorn rope,
My tree a captive in your window bay
Has lost its footing on my mountain slope
And lost the stars of heaven, may, oh, may
The symbol star it lifts against your ceiling
Help me accept its fate with Christmas feeling.

Robert Frost

THE CULTIVATION OF CHRISTMAS TREES

There are several attitudes towards Christmas,
Some of which we may disregard;
The social, the torpid, the patently commercial,
The rowdy (the pubs being open till midnight),
And the childish—which is not that of the child
For whom the candle is a star, and the gilded angel
Spreading its wings at the summit of the tree
Is not only a decoration, but an angel.
The child wonders at the Christmas Tree:
Let him continue in the spirit of wonder
At the Feast as an event not accepted as a pretext;
So that the glittering rapture, the amazement
Of the first-remembered Christmas Tree,
So that the surprises, delight in new possessions
(Each one with its peculiar and exciting smell),
The expectation of the goose or turkey
And the expected awe on its appearance,
So that the reverence and the gaiety,
May not be forgotten in later experience,
In the bored habituation, the fatigue, the tedium,
The awareness of death, the consciousness of failure,
Or in the piety of the convert
Which may be tainted with a self-conceit
Displeasing to God, and disrespectful to the children
(And here I remember also with gratitude
St Lucy, her carol, and her crown of fire):
So that before the end, the eightieth Christmas
(By 'eightieth' meaning whichever is the last)
The accumulated memories of annual emotion
May be concentrated into a great joy

Which shall be also a great fear, as on the occasion
When fear came upon every soul:
Because the beginning shall remind us of the end
And the first coming of the second coming.

T. S. Eliot

Christmas Eve

CHRISTMAS EVE IN PETROGRAD

On Christmas Eve, late in the evening, I went into a church. It was my favourite church in Petrograd, rising at the English Prospect end of the Quay, with its white rounded towers pure and quiet and modest.

I had been depressed all day. I had not been well, and the weather was harsh, a bitterly cold driving wind beating down the streets and stroking the ice of the canal into a dull grey colour. Christmas seemed to lift into sharper, bitterer irony the ghastly horrors of this endless war. Last Christmas I had been too ill to care, and the Christmas before I had been at the front, when the war had been young and full of hope . . . I entered the church and found the service was over. I passed through the aisle into the little rounded cup of dark and gold where the altars were. Here there were still collected a company of people, kneeling, some of them, in front of the candles, others standing there, motionless like statues, their hands folded, gazing before them. The candles flung a mist of dim embroidery upon the walls and, within the mist, the dark figures of the priests moved to and fro. An old priest with long white hair was standing behind a desk close to me, and reading a long prayer in an unswerving monotonous voice. There was the scent of candles and cold stone and hot human breath in the little place. The tawdry gilt of the Ikons glittered in the candle-light, and an echo of the cold wind creeping up the long dark aisle blew the light about so that the gilt was like flashing, piercing eyes. I wrapped my Shuba closely about me, and stood there lost in a hazy indefinite dream.

I was comforted and touched by the placid, mild, kindly faces of those standing near me. 'No evil here . . .' I thought. 'Only ignorance, and for that others are responsible.'

I was lost in my dream and I did not know what I was dreaming. The priest's voice went on, and the lights flickered, and it was as though someone, a long way off, were trying to give me a message that it was important that I should hear.

Hugh Walpole

CHRISTMAS EVE AT SEA

A wind is rustling 'south and soft',
   Cooing a quiet country tune,
The calm sea sighs, and far aloft
   The sails are ghostly in the moon.

Unquiet ripples lisp and purr,
   A block there pipes and chirps i' the sheave,
The wheel-ropes jar, the reef-points stir
   Faintly—and it is Christmas Eve.

The hushed sea seems to hold her breath,
   And o'er the giddy, swaying spars,
Silent and excellent as Death,
   The dim blue skies are bright with stars.

Dear God—they shone in Palestine
   Like this, and yon pale moon serene
Looked down among the lowing kine
   On Mary and the Nazarene.

The angels called from deep to deep,
   The burning heavens felt the thrill,
Startling the flocks of silly sheep,
   And lonely shepherds on the hill.

Tonight beneath the dripping bows
   Where flashing bubbles burst and throng,
The bow-wash murmurs and sighs and soughs
   A message from the angels' song.

The moon goes nodding down the west,
  The drowsy helmsman strikes the bell;
Rex Judaeorum natus est,
  I charge you, brothers, sing Nowell, Nowell,
Rex Judaeorum natus est.

John Masefield

CHRISTMAS EVE AT DINGLEY DELL

It was a pleasant thing to see Mr Pickwick in the centre of the group [under the mistletoe], now pulled this way and then that, and first kissed on the chin, and then on the nose, and then on the spectacles, and to hear the peals of laughter which were raised on every side; but it was a still more pleasant thing to see Mr Pickwick, blinded shortly afterwards with a silk handkerchief, falling up against the wall, and scrambling into corners, and going through all the mysteries of blind-man's buff, with the utmost relish for the game, until at last he caught one of the poor relations, and then to evade the blind-man himself, which he did with a nimbleness and agility that elicited the admiration and applause of all beholders. . . . When they were all tired of blind-man's buff, there was a great game of snap-dragon, and when fingers enough were burned with that, and all the raisins were gone, they sat down by the huge fire of blazing logs to a substantial supper, and a mighty bowl of wassail, something smaller than an ordinary wash-house copper, in which the hot apples were hissing and bubbling with a rich look, and a jolly sound, that were perfectly irresistible.

'This,' said Mr Pickwick, looking round him, 'this is, indeed, comfort.'

'Our invariable custom,' replied Mr Wardle. 'Everybody sits down with us on Christmas Eve, as you see them now—servants and all; and here we wait, until the clock strikes twelve, to usher Christmas in, and beguile the time with forfeits and old stories. Trundle, my boy, rake up the fire.'

Charles Dickens

Christmas Day

ON THE MORNING OF CHRIST'S NATIVITY

This is the month, and this the happy morn,
  Wherein the Son of Heaven's Eternal King,
Of wedded maid and virgin mother born,
  Our great redemption from above did bring;
For so the holy sages once did sing,
  That he our deadly forfeit should release,
And with his Father work us a perpetual peace.

John Milton

THE BURNING BABE

As I in hoary winter's night
  Stood shivering in the snow,
Surprised I was with sudden heat
  Which made my heart to glow;
And lifting up a fearful eye
  To view what fire was near,
A pretty babe all burning bright
  Did in the air appear;
Who, scorchèd with excessive heat,
  Such floods of tears did shed,
As though His floods should quench His flames,
  Which with His tears were bred:
'Alas!' quoth He, 'but newly born
  In fiery heats I fry,
Yet none approach to warm their hearts
  Or feel my fire but I.'

'My faultless breast the furnace is;
  The fuel, wounding thorns;
Love is the fire, and sighs the smoke;
  The ashes, shames and scorns;
The fuel Justice layeth on,
  And Mercy blows the coals,
The metal in this furnace wrought
  Are men's defilèd souls:
For which, as now on fire I am
  To work them to their good,
So will I melt into a bath,
  To wash them in my blood.'
With this He vanish'd out of sight
  And swiftly shrunk away,
And straight I callèd unto mind
  That it was Christmas Day.

Robert Southwell

PERILOUS TIMES

1657, December 20. I went with my wife and company to London to celebrate Christmas Day. Mr Gunning was preaching at Exeter Chapel on 7 Micah 2. Sermon ended. As he was giving us the Holy Sacrament, the chapel was surrounded with soldiers. All the communicants and assembly surprised and kept prisoner by them; some in the house, others carried away. It fell to my share to be confined to a room in the house, where yet permitted to dine with the master of it, the Countess of Dorset, Lady Hatton, and some others of quality who invited me. In the afternoon came Colonel Whaly, Goffe, and others from Whitehall, to examine us one by one. Some they committed to the Martial [an officer], some to prison, some committed. When I came before them, they took my name and abode, examined me, why, contrary to an Ordinance made that none should any longer observe the superstitious time of the Nativity (so esteemed by them) I durst offend.

*John Evelyn**

*John Evelyn kept his diary from 1641 to 1697. He was, all his life, a strong Royalist and a devout churchman. 1657 was a time of Puritan rule, when Church of England priests were forbidden to hold services.

MR PEPYS'S CHRISTMAS DAY

[*25th December 1662*]

Had a pleasant walk to White Hall, where I intended to have received the communion with the family, but I come a little too late. So I walked up into the house, and spent my time looking over pictures, particularly the ships in Henry the VIIIth's Voyage to Bullaen; marking the great difference between those built then and now. By and by down to the chapel again, where Bishop Morely preached. . . . Methought he made but a poor sermon, but long. . . . He did much press us to joy in these publick days of joy, and to hospitality. But one that stood by whispered in my ear that the Bishop do not spend one groat to the poor himself. The sermon done a good anthem followed with vialls, and the King come down to receive the Sacrament.

Samuel Pepys

AT SEA, 1675

Christmas Day we'll keepe thus: At four in the morning our trumpeters all doe flatt their trumpets, and begin at our Captain's Cabin, and thence to all the officers' and gentlemen's Cabins; playing a levite at each cabin door, and bidding good morrow, wishing a Merry Christmas.

After they goe to their station, viz. on the poope, and sound three levites in honour of the morning. At ten we goe to prayers and sermon; text Zaac. IX.9.

Our Captain had all his officers and gentlemen to dinner with him where wee had excellent good fayre; a ribb of beefe, plumb puddings, minct pyes, &c., and plenty of good wines of severall sorts; dranke healths to the King, to our wives and friends, and ended the day with much civill myrth.

*Henry Teonge**

*The Revd Henry Teonge, Rector of Alcester, Warwickshire, left his parish at the age of fifty-four and went to sea as a chaplain in order to support his starving family. He was so poor that he pawned practically everything he had.

CHRISTMAS DAY, 1784

December 25—very bright morn. Trees beautifully powdered with Rime, more severity of Freezing than any since the first beginning, very little wind but ye Air amazingly keen. Sound of bells heard from all ye Villages on every side. Sac^{rt}. at Fyfield. Riding not unpleasant over ye open Fields and Downs. Trees powdered most amazingly by ye Rime make a very picturesque appearance at Tidworth. Pump frozen in ye Wash House! so that ye Frost tho not quite so cold as ye 2 first days yet operates more strongly within doors. Winter reigns in all its rigour and yet ye Sun shines unusually warm p.m. every day which seems to destroy every sort of broad leaved evergreen. Holly and Ivy leaves brt. to decorate the churches and houses, seem scorched and blasted.

Henry White

ON CHRISTMAS DAY

Shake off thy sloth, my drowsy soul, awake;
With angels sing
Unto thy king,
And pleasant music make;
Thy lute, thy harp, or else thy heartstrings take,
And with thy music let thy sense awake.
See how each one of the other calls
To fix his ivy on the walls,
Transplanted there it seems to grow
As if it rooted were below;
Thus he, who is thy king,
Makes winter, spring.

'Twas thou gav'st us cause for fine attires;
Ev'n though, O king,
As in the spring,
Dost warm us with thy fires
Of love; thy blood hath brought us new desires;
Thy righteousness doth clothe with new attires.
Both fine and fresh let me appear
This day divine, to close the year;
Among the rest let me be seen
A living branch and always-green,
Think it a pleasant thing
Thy praise to sing.

Thomas Traherne

THIS DAY

Natus est vobis hodie Salvator

Why, saith the son of Sirach, doth
  One day excel,
When any other day might seem
  To do as well?
The sun arises and it sets
  On ev'ry day,
And season after season comes
  And goes its way;
All things are full of weariness,
  All things the same,
The seeming new itself was old
  Before it came.

Yet to this world of weariness,
  So sad, you say,
There came a Babe with Christmas joy,
  Upon a day
—Upon a day—and still we ring
  The Christmas bells,
And hold that over other days
  One day excels.

Sir Frederick Still

Celebration

A PSALM FOR CHRISTMAS DAY MORNING

Fairest of morning lights appear,
Thou blest and gaudy day,
On whom was born our Saviour dear,
Make haste and come away.

This day prevents His day of doom,
His mercy now is nigh;
The mighty God of Love is come,
The Dayspring from on high.

Behold the Great Creator makes
Himself a house of clay,
A robe of Virgin flesh He takes
Which He will wear for aye.

Hark, hark, the wise Eternal Word
Like a weak infant cries;
In form of servant is the Lord,
And God in cradle lies.

This wonder struck the world amazed,
It shook the starry frame;
Squadrons of Spirits stood and gazed,
Then down in troops they came.

Glad shepherds ran to view this sight,
A choir of Angels sings,
And Eastern Sages with delight
Adore this King of Kings.

Join then all hearts that are not stone,
And all our voices prove,
To celebrate this Holy One,
The God of Peace and Love.

Thomas Pestel

RING THE BELLS, THE CHRISTMAS BELLS

Ring the bells, the Christmas bells;
  Chime out the wondrous story!
First in song on angel tongues
  It came from realms of glory—
Peace on earth, good-will to men,
  Angelic voices ringing;
Christ the Lord to earth has come,
  His glorious message bringing.

Chorus:
  Ring the merry Christmas bells:
    Chime out the wondrous story:
  Glory be to God on high;
    For evermore be glory!

Wise men hastened from the east,
  To bring their richest treasure—
Gold, and myrrh, and frankincense,
  And jewels without measure.
Him they sought, although a King,
  They found in birthplace lowly:
There within a manger lay
  The Babe so pure and holy.

Earthly crowns were not for Him;
  He came God's love revealing:
On the cross He died for us,
  His blood forgiveness sealing.

'Tis the Saviour promised long;
  Ring out your loudest praises!
Every heart this happy day
  Its grateful anthems raises.

Agnes Burney

HEAP ON MORE WOOD

Heap on more wood!—the wind is chill;
But let it whistle as it will,
We'll keep our Christmas merry still.
Each age had deem'd the new-born year
The fittest time for festal cheer;
Even, heathen yet, the savage Dane
At Iol more deep the mead did drain;
High on the beach his galleys drew,
And feasted all his pirate crew. . . .

And well our Christian sires of old
Loved when the year its course had roll'd,
And brought blithe Christmas back again,
With all his hospitable train.
Domestic and religious rite
Gave honour to the holy night;
On Christmas Eve the bells were rung;
On Christmas Eve the mass was sung:
That only night in all the year
Saw the stoled priest the chalice rear.
The damsel donn'd her kirtle sheen;
The hall was dress'd with holly green;
Forth to the wood did merry-men go,
To gather in the mistletoe.
Then open'd wide the baron's hall
To vassal, tenant, serf, and all;
Power laid his rod of rule aside,
And Ceremony doff'd his pride. . . .

The fire, with well-dried logs supplied,
Went roaring up the chimney wide;
The huge hall-table's oaken face,
Scrubb'd till it shone, the day to grace,
Bore then upon its massive board
No mark to part the squire and lord.
Then was brought in the lusty brawn,
By old blue-coated serving-men;
Then the grim boar's head frown'd on high,
Crested with bays and rosemary. . . .
The wassel round, in good brown bowls
Garnish'd with ribbons, blithely trowls.
There the huge sirloin reek'd; hard by
Plum-porridge stood, and Christmas pie;
Nor fail'd old Scotland to produce,
At such high tide, her savoury goose.
Then came the merry maskers in,
And carols roar'd with blithesome din;
If unmelodious was the song,
It was a hearty note, and strong.
Who lists may in their mumming see
Traces of ancient mystery. . . .
A Christmas gambol oft could cheer
The poor man's heart through half the year.

Sir Walter Scott

MERRY PIPING TIME OF CHRISTMAS

Close the shutters, and draw the curtains together, and pile fresh wood upon the hearth! Let us have, for once, an innocent *auto-da-fé*. Let the hoarded corks be brought forth, and branches of crackling laurel. Place the wine and fruit and the hot chestnuts upon the table. And now, good folks and children, bring your chairs round to the blazing fire. Put some of those rosy apples upon your plates. We'll drink one glass of bright sherry 'To our absent friends' and then talk a little about Christmas.

It is the happiest time of the year. It is the season of mirth and cold weather. It is the time when Christmas-boxes and jokes are given; when mistletoe, and red-berried laurel, and soups, and sliding, and schoolboys, prevail; when the country is illuminated by fires and bright faces; and the town is radiant with laughing children. . . . But look! what thing is this, awful and coloured like the rainbow,—blue, and red, and glistening yellow? Its vest is sky-tinctured! The edges of its garments are like the sun! Is it

A faery vision
Of some gay creature of the element,
That in the colours of the rainbow lives,
And plays i' the plighted clouds?

No;—it is the Beadle of St—'s! How Christmas and consolatory he looks! How redolent of good cheer he is! He is a cornu-copia— an abundance! What pudding-sleeves!—what a collar, red and like a beef-steak, is his. He is a walking refreshment! He looks like a whole parish,—full, important,—but untaxed. The children of charity gaze at him with a modest smile, the straggling boys look on him with confidence. They do not pocket their marbles. They do not fly from the familiar gutter. This is a red-letter day; and the cane is reserved for to-morrow.

Oh! merry piping time for Christmas! Never let us permit thee to degenerate into distant courtesies and formal salutations. But let us shake our friends and familiars by the hands, as our fathers and their fathers did. Let them all come around us, and let us count how many the year has added to our circle.

Charles Lamb

SIR ROGER DE COVERLEY

I was no sooner come into Gray's Inn walks, but I heard my friend upon the terrace hemming twice or thrice to himself with great vigour, for he loves to clear his pipes in good air (to make use of his own phrase), and is not a little pleased with anyone who takes notice of the strength which he still exerts in morning hems. I was touched with a secret joy at the sight of the good old man, who before he saw me was engaged in conversation with a beggar man that had asked an alms of him. I could hear my friend chide him for not finding out some work; but at the same time saw him put his hand into his pocket and give him sixpence.

Our salutations were very hearty on both sides, consisting of many kinds of shakes of the hand, and several affectionate looks which we cast upon one another. He afterwards fell into an account of the diversions which had passed in his house during the holidays; for Sir Roger, after the laudable custom of his ancestors, always keeps open house at Christmas. I learned from him, that he had killed eight fat hogs for this season; that he had dealt about his chines very liberally amongst his neighbours; and that in particular he had sent a string of hog's-puddings with a pack of cards to every poor family in the parish. 'I have often thought', says Sir Roger, 'it happens very well that Christmas should fall out in the middle of winter. It is the most dead and uncomfortable time of the year, when the poor people would suffer very much from their poverty and cold, if they had not good cheer, warm fires, and Christmas gambols to support them. I love to rejoice their poor hearts at this season, and to see the whole village merry in my great hall. I allow a double quantity of malt to my small beer, and set it a-running for twelve days to every one that calls for it. I have always a piece of cold beef and a mince-pie upon the table, and am wonderfully pleased to see my tenants pass away a whole evening in playing their innocent tricks, and smutting one another. Our friend Will Wimble is as merry as any of them, and shows a thousand roguish tricks upon these occasions.'

I was very much delighted with the reflection of my old friend, which carried so much goodness in it.

Joseph Addison

THE SQUIRE'S CHRISTMAS BANQUET

The dinner was served up in the great hall, where the Squire always held his Christmas banquet. A blazing, crackling fire of logs had been heaped on to warm the spacious apartment, and the flame went wreathing and sparkling up the wide-mouthed chimney. We were ushered into the banqueting scene with the sound of minstrelsy, the old harper being seated on a stool beside the fireplace, and twanging his instrument with a vast deal more power than melody. Never did Christmas board display a more goodly and gracious assembly of countenances; those who were not handsome were at least happy; and happiness is a rare improver of your hard-favoured visage.

The parson said grace, which was not a short familiar one, such as is commonly addressed to the Deity in these unceremonious days; but a long, courtly, well-worded one of the ancient school. There was now a pause as if something was expected; when suddenly the butler entered the hall with some degree of bustle; he was attended by a servant on each side with a large wax light, and bore a silver dish, on which was an enormous pig's head decorated with rosemary, with a lemon in its mouth, which was placed with great formality at the head of the table. I confess the parade with which so odd a dish was introduced somewhat perplexed me, until I gathered from the conversation of the Squire and the parson that it was meant to represent the bringing in of the boar's head: a dish formerly served up with much ceremony, and the sound of minstrelsy and song at great tables on Christmas Day.

The table was literally loaded with good cheer, and presented an epitome of country abundance in this season of overflowing larders. A distinguished post was allotted to 'ancient sirloin' as mine host termed it; being, as he added, 'the standard of our old English hospitality, and a joint of goodly presence, and full of expectation'.

When the cloth was removed the butler brought in a huge silver vessel of curious workmanship, which he placed before the Squire. Its appearance was hailed with acclamation; being the Wassail Bowl, so renowned in Christmas festivity. The contents had been prepared by the Squire himself . . . and it was a potation that might well make the heart of a toper leap within him; being compounded of the richest wines, highly spiced and sweetened, with roasted apples bobbing about the surface.

Having raised it to his lips with a hearty wish of a merry Christmas to all present, the Squire sent it brimming round the board for every one to follow his example according to the primitive style; pronouncing it 'the ancient fountain of good feeling, where all hearts meet together'. There was much laughing and rallying as the honest emblem of Christmas joviality circulated, and was kissed rather coyly by the ladies.

Washington Irving

AN ODE ON THE BIRTH OF OUR SAVIOUR

In numbers, and but these few,
I sing Thy birth, O Jesu!
Thou pretty baby, born here,
With sup'rabundant scorn here;
Who for Thy princely port here,
Hadst for Thy place
Of birth a base
Out-stable for Thy court here.

Instead of near enclosures
Of interwoven osiers,
Instead of fragrant posies
Of daffodils and roses,
Thy cradle, Kingly Stranger,
As Gospel tells,
Was nothing else
But here a homely manger.

The Jews they did disdain Thee,
But we will entertain Thee,
With glories to await here,
Upon Thy princely state here;
And more for love than pity,
From year to year,
We'll make Thee, here,
A free-born of our city.

Robert Herrick

THE SHEPHERD AND THE KING

The Shepherd and the King,
The Angel and the Ass,
They heard Sweet Mary sing
When her joy was come to pass:
They heard Sweet Mary sing
To the Baby on her knee,
Sing again, Sweet Mary,
And we will sing with thee!

Earth, bear a berry!
Heaven, bear a light!
Man, make you merry
On Christmas night.

The oxen in the stall,
The sheep upon the hill,
They are waking all
To hear Sweet Mary still.
The Baby is a Child
And the Child is running free,
Sing again, Sweet Mary
And we will sing with thee!

The people in the land,
So many million strong,
All silently do stand
To hear Sweet Mary's song.
The Child he is a Man,
And the Man hangs on a tree!
Sing again, Sweet Mary,
And we will sing with thee!

The Stars that are so old,
The grass that is so young,
They listen in the cold
To hear Sweet Mary's tongue.
The Man's the Son of God
And in Heaven walketh He,
Sing again, Sweet Mary,
And we will sing with thee!

Anonymous

THE CRATCHITS' CHRISTMAS DINNER

Such a bustle ensued that you might have thought a goose the rarest of all birds; a feathered phenomenon, to which a black swan was a matter of course—and in truth it was something very like it in that house. Mrs Cratchit made the gravy (ready beforehand in a little saucepan) hissing hot; Master Peter mashed the potatoes with incredible vigour; Miss Belinda sweetened up the apple-sauce; Martha dusted the hot plates; Bob took Tiny Tim beside him in a tiny corner at the table; the two young Cratchits set chairs for everybody, not forgetting themselves, and mounting guard upon their posts, crammed spoons into their mouths, lest they should shriek for goose before their turn came to be helped. At last the dishes were set on, and grace was said. It was succeeded by a breathless pause, as Mrs Cratchit, looking slowly all along the carving-knife, prepared to plunge it into the breast; but when she did, and when the long expected gush of stuffing issued forth, one murmur of delight arose all round the board, and even Tiny Tim, excited by the two young Cratchits, beat on the table with the handle of his knife, and feebly cried Hurrah!

There never was such a goose. Bob said he didn't believe there ever was such a goose cooked. Its tenderness and flavour, size and cheapness, were themes of universal admiration. Eked out by apple-sauce and mashed potatoes, it was a sufficient dinner for the whole family . . . But now, the plates being changed by Miss Belinda, Mrs Cratchit left the room alone—too nervous to bear witnesses—to take the pudding up and bring it in. . . . Hallo! A great deal of steam! The pudding was out of the copper. A smell like a washing-day! That was the cloth. A smell like an eating-house and a pastry-cook's next door to each other, with a laundress's next door to that! That was the pudding! In half a minute Mrs Cratchit entered—flushed, but smiling proudly—with the pudding like a speckled cannon-ball, so hard and firm, and blazing in half of half-a-quartern of ignited brandy, and bedight with Christmas holly stuck into the top.

Oh, a wonderful pudding! Bob Cratchit said, and calmly too, that he regarded it as the greatest success achieved by Mrs Cratchit since their marriage. Mrs Cratchit said that now the weight was off her mind, she would confess she had had her doubts about the quantity of flour. Everybody had something to say about it, but nobody said or thought it was at all a small pudding for a large family. It would have been a flat heresy to do so. Any Cratchit would have blushed to hint at such a thing.

Charles Dickens

THE VICTORIAN CHRISTMAS PANTOMIME

Twenty-Eighth December, 1860.

I pass my time here (I am staying here alone) in working, taking physic, and taking a stall at the Theatre every night. On Boxing Night I was at Covent Garden. A dull pantomime was 'worked' (as we say) better than I ever saw a heavy piece worked on a first night, until suddenly and without a moment's warning, every scene on that immense stage fell over on its face, and disclosed Chaos by Gaslight behind! There never was such a business—about sixty people who were on the stage being extinguished in the most remarkable manner. Not a soul was hurt. In the uproar, some mooncalf rescued a porter pot, six feet high (one of which the clown had been drinking when the accident happened), and stood it on the cushion of the lowest Proscenium Box, P.S., beside a lady and gentleman, who were dreadfully ashamed of it. The moment the House knew that nobody was injured, they directed their whole attention to this gigantic porter pot in its genteel position (the lady and gentleman trying to hide behind it), and roared with laughter. When a modest footman came from behind the curtain to clear it, and took it up in his arms like a Brobdingnagian Baby, we all laughed more than ever we had laughed in our lives. I don't know why. . . .

The poor actors waylay me in Bow Street to represent their necessities; and I often see one cut down a court when he beholds me coming—cut round Drury Lane to face me—and come up towards me near this door in the freshest and most accidental way; as if I was the last person he expected to see on the surface of this globe. The other day, there thus appeared before me (simultaneously with a scent of rum in the air) one aged and greasy man, with a pair of pumps under his arm. He said he thought if he could get down to somewhere (I think it was Newcastle), he would get 'taken on' as Pantaloon, the existing Pantaloon being 'a stick, sir—a mere muff.' I observed that I was sorry times were so bad with him. 'Mr Dickens, you know our profession, Sir—no one knows it better, Sir—there is no right feeling in it. I was Harlequin on your own circuit, Sir, for five-and-thirty years, and was displaced by a boy, Sir—a boy!'

Charles Dickens

PRESENT MIRTH AND PAST AFFECTION

A rich hilarity drew them all together that day. They loved the sound of each other's voices; they laughed on the least provocation; by evening, the young men showed a tendency toward horse play. There was a late dinner, dominated by the largest turkey Alayne had ever seen. There was a black and succulent plum pudding with brandy sauce. There were native sherry and port. The Fennels were there; the two daughters of the retired admiral; and lonely little Miss Pink, the organist. Mr Fennel proposed Grandmother's health, in a toast so glowing with metaphor and prickling with wit that she suggested that if he were three sheets in the wind on Sunday he would preach a sermon worth hearing. . . .

A great platter of raisins smothered in flaming brandy was carried in by Rags, wearing his exalted air of an acolyte.

Seeing Rags' hard face in that strange light carried Renny as in a dream to another very different scene. He saw Rags bent over a saucepan in a dug-out in France, wearing a filthy uniform, and, oddly enough, that same expression. But why, he could not remember. He had picked Rags up in France. Renny looked up into his eyes with a smile, and a queer worshipping grin spread over Rags' grim hardbitten face.

Mazo de la Roche

CHRISTMAS MINIATURE

I see a great white space, in the midst of it Christmas,
  A shrine of coloured candles on the King's highway;
And He who sits in state is our own quiet Jesus,
  And she who lights the tallow-wicks, May.

For Mary hath her roses and bluebells in December,
  All dewy is her gown with Spring.
I see it so plain in the Yuletide ember,
  Round her the merry birds sing;

One of them has feathers like a little yellow-hammer,
  One of them is azure as the day;
And a green thrush hops on a white woolly lamb;
  While round them the angels play.

On sackbut and psaltery and castanets,
  On tibia and tambourine and lyre.
And seven little alabaster minarets
  See I, too, in the forest of the fire.

Herbert Palmer

The Promise of Christmas

THAT HOLY THING

They all were looking for a king
To slay their foes and lift them high:
Thou cam'st, a little baby thing
That made a woman cry.

O Son of Man, to right my lot
Naught but Thy presence can avail;
Yet on the road Thy wheels are not,
Nor on the sea Thy sail!

My how or when Thou wilt not heed,
But come down Thine own secret stair,
That Thou mayst answer all my need—
Yea, every bygone prayer.

George MacDonald

CRADLED IN A MANGER

Cradled in a manger, meanly
  Laid the Son of Man His head;
Sleeping His first earthly slumber
  Where the oxen had been fed.
Happy were those shepherds listening
  To the holy angel's word;
Happy they, within that stable,
  Worshipping their infant Lord.

Happy all who hear the message
  Of His coming from above;
Happier still who hail His coming,
  And with praises greet His love.
Blessèd Saviour, Christ most holy,
  In a manger Thou didst rest;
Canst Thou stoop again, yet lower,
  And abide within my breast?

Evil things are there before Thee:
  In the heart, where they have fed,
Wilt Thou pitifully enter,
  Son of Man, and lay Thy head?
Enter, then, O Christ most holy;
  Make a Christmas in my heart;
Make a heaven of my manger;
  It is heaven where Thou art.

And to those who never listened
  To the message of Thy birth,
Who have winter, but no Christmas
  Bringing them Thy peace on earth,

Send to these the joyful tidings;
By all people, in each home,
Be there heard the Christmas anthem,
'Praise to God, the Christ has come!'

G. Stringer Rowe

THE HOUSE OF CHRISTMAS

There fared a mother driven forth,
Out of an inn to roam;
In the place where she was homeless
All men are at home.
The crazy stable close at hand,
With shaking timber and shifting sand,
Grew a stronger thing to abide and stand
Than the square stones of Rome.

For men are homesick in their homes,
And strangers under the sun,
And they lay their heads in a foreign land
Whenever the day is done.
Here we have battle and blazing eyes
And chance and honour and high surprise,
But our homes are under miraculous skies
Where the yule tale was begun.

A child in a foul stable,
Where the beasts feed and foam;
Only where He was homeless
Are you and I at home;
We have hands that fashion and heads that know,
But our hearts we lost—how long ago!
In a place no chart nor ship can show
Under the sky's dome.

This world is wild as an old wives' tale,
And strange the plain things are,
The earth is enough and the air is enough
For our wonder and our war;

But our rest is as far as the fire-drake swings
And our peace is put in impossible things
Where clashed and thundered unthinkable wings
Round an incredible star.

To an open house in the evening
Home shall men come,
To an older place than Eden
And a taller town than Rome.
To the end of the way of the wandering star,
To the things that cannot be and that are,
To the place where God was homeless
And all men are at home.

G. K. Chesterton

THE OXEN

Christmas Eve, and twelve of the clock.
   'Now they are all on their knees,'
An Elder said as we sat in a flock
   By the embers in hearthside ease.

We pictured the meek mild creatures where
   They dwelt in their strawy pen,
Nor did it occur to one of us there
   To doubt they were kneeling then.

So fair a fancy few would weave
   In these years! Yet, I feel,
If someone said on Christmas Eve,
   'Come; see the oxen kneel

'In the lonely barton by yonder coomb*
   Our childhood used to know,'
I should go with him in the gloom,
   Hoping it might be so.

Thomas Hardy

*Farmyard in a hollow

YULE-TIDE FIRES

Cleanse with the burning log of oak
The canker of thy care,
Deck with the scarlet-berried bough
The temple of the fair;
Spread pure-white linen for a feast,
Perchance some guest may share.

Give forth thy gold and silver coins,
For they were lent to thee;
Put out to usury thy dross,
One talent gaineth three.
Perchance the hungered and the poor
May pray to God for thee.

Once a pale star rose in the East
For watching herds to see,
And weakness came to Bethlehem,
And strength to Galilee.
Perchance, if thou dost keep thy tryst,
A star may rise for thee.

Anonymous

CHRISTMAS

The bells of waiting Advent ring,
   The Tortoise stove is lit again
And lamp-oil light across the night
   Has caught the streaks of winter rain
In many a stained-glass window sheen
From Crimson Lake to Hooker's Green.

The holly in the windy hedge
   And round the Manor House the yew
Will soon be stripped to deck the ledge,
   The altar, font and arch and pew,
So that the villagers can say
'The church looks nice' on Christmas Day.

Provincial public houses blaze
   And Corporation tramcars clang,
On lighted tenements I gaze
   Where paper decorations hang,
And bunting in the red Town Hall
Says 'Merry Christmas to you all.'

And London shops on Christmas Eve
   Are strung with silver bells and flowers
As hurrying clerks the City leave
   To pigeon-haunted classic towers,
And marbled clouds go scudding by
The many-steepled London sky.

And girls in slacks remember Dad,
   And oafish louts remember Mum,
And sleepless children's hearts are glad,
   And Christmas-morning bells say 'Come!'
Even to shining ones who dwell
Safe in the Dorchester Hotel.

And is it true? And is it true,
   This most tremendous tale of all,
Seen in a stained-glass window's hue,
   A Baby in an ox's stall?
The Maker of the stars and sea
Become a Child on earth for me?

And is it true? For if it is,
   No loving fingers tying strings
Around those tissued fripperies,
   The sweet and silly Christmas things,
Bath salts and inexpensive scent
And hideous tie so kindly meant,

No love that in a family dwells,
   No carolling in frosty air,
Nor all the steeple-shaking bells
   Can with this single Truth compare—
That God was Man in Palestine
And lives today in Bread and Wine.

John Betjeman

DIVINE CHARITY: DIVINE ART

I was talking a few years ago with a relative of Arnold Bennett who told me of many sweet and tender things the popular novelist had done for his own people, and this point of the conversation was the care with which Arnold Bennett so often staged his surprises, and the art with which he decorated his gifts. It was a pleasing glimpse of the well-known writer, and I warm to him whenever I recall the story.

To make a gift is an impulse of divine charity; to make it perfectly is a divine art. God made an art of His gift when He placed it on the breast of Mary in the little town of Bethlehem.

It is a far cry from Bethlehem to Calvary—as far as from the toys of the nursery to the dark chambers of torture. But it is Christ who spans these extremes we worship, the child of the carol and the Man of Sorrows, which is to say, all humanity, all its vast experiences gathered in a single life . . . The Christ of Christmas sets me amid the tender humanities; the cry of the Man on the Cross brings me to the redemptive pains, the travail of the soul of the world, which is the cost of our deliverance into the Kingdom of Heaven.

Christianity is lowly enough, human, and intimate enough, for all that. It comes to add security to things already safe, to give assurance to the things already assured, to make us see the things we have always seen; in other words, to give us the eyes of a child, to consecrate the commonplace, to make plain the obvious, to turn the usual into a miracle of divine love. It begins with a carol, sweet clean music; with shepherds, the symbol of simplicity; and if there are wise men in the picture, they are certainly not college dons. And that simple, human note remains through the whole story, even to the Cross, where Christ turns in His agony to commend His mother to the care of another with tenderest grace.

A. E. Whitham

The Kings

THE WISE WISE-MEN

Now when Jesus was born in Bethlehem of Judea in the days of Herod the king, behold, there came wise men from the east to Jerusalem, saying, Where is He that is born King of the Jews? for we have seen his star in the east and are come to worship him.

When Herod the king had heard these things he was troubled, and all Jerusalem with him. And when he had gathered all the chief priests and scribes of the people together, he demanded of them where Christ should be born. And they said unto him, In Bethlehem of Judea; for thus it is written by the prophet, And thou Bethlehem in the land of Judah, art not the least among the princes of Judah: for out of thee shall come a Governor, that shall rule my people Israel.

Then Herod, when he had privily called the wise men, inquired of them diligently what time the star appeared. And he sent them to Bethlehem, and said, Go and search diligently for the young child; and when ye have found him, bring me word again, that I may come and worship him also.

When they had heard the king, they departed; and lo, the star, which they saw in the east, went before them, till it came and stood over where the young child was. When they saw the star, they rejoiced with exceeding great joy. And when they were come into the house, they saw the young child with Mary his mother, and fell down, and worshipped him: and when they had opened their treasures, they presented unto him gifts; gold, and frankincense, and myrrh.

And being warned of God in a dream that they should not return to Herod, they departed into their own country another way.

St Matthew

JOURNEY OF THE MAGI

'A cold coming we had of it,
Just the worst time of the year
For a journey, and such a long journey:
The ways deep and the weather sharp,
The very dead of winter.'
And the camels galled, sore-footed, refractory,
Lying down in the melting snow.
There were times we regretted
The summer palaces on slopes, the terraces,
And the silken girls bringing sherbet.
Then the camel men cursing and grumbling
And running away, and wanting their liquor and women,
And the night-fires going out, and the lack of shelters,
And the cities hostile and the towns unfriendly
And the villages dirty and charging high prices:
A hard time we had of it.
At the end we preferred to travel all night,
Sleeping in snatches,
With the voices singing in our ears, saying
That this was all folly.

Then at dawn we came down to a temperate valley,
Wet, below the snow line, smelling of vegetation;
With a running stream and a water-mill beating the
darkness,
And three trees on the low sky,
And an old white horse galloped away in the meadow.
Then we came to a tavern with vine-leaves over the
lintel,
Six hands at an open door dicing for pieces of silver,
And feet kicking the empty wine-skins.
But there was no information, and so we continued
And arrived at evening, not a moment too soon
Finding the place; it was (you may say) satisfactory.

All this was a long time ago, I remember,
And I would do it again, but set down
This set down
This: were we led all that way for
Birth or Death? There was a Birth, certainly,
We had evidence and no doubt. I had seen birth and
death,
But had thought they were different; this Birth was
Hard and bitter agony for us, like Death, our death.
We returned to our places, these Kingdoms,
But no longer at ease here, in the old dispensation,
With an alien people clutching their gods.
I should be glad of another death.

T. S. Eliot

KINGS CAME RIDING

Kings came riding,
 One, two and three,
Over the desert
 And over the sea.

One in a ship
 With a silver mast;
The fishermen wondered
 As he went past.

One on a horse
 With a saddle of gold;
The children came running
 To behold.

One came walking,
 Over the sand,
With a casket of treasure
 Held in his hand.

All the people
 Said, 'Where go they?'
But the kings went forward
 All through the day.

Night came on
 As those kings went by;
They shone like the gleaming
 Stars in the sky.

Charles Williams

THE THREE DARK MAGI

He groped his way through the dark suburb. The houses stood, snapped off, against the sky. There was no moon and the pavement was startled by his belated tread. Then he found an old fence. He kicked it with his foot till a rotten lath heaved a sigh and broke off. The wood smelt over-ripe and sweet. Through the dark suburb he groped his way back. There were no stars.

As he opened the door (it cried as he did so, the door) the pale blue eyes of his wife looked towards him. They came from a tired face. Her breath hung white in the room, it was so cold. He bent his bony knee and broke the wood. The wood sighed. Then there was a sweet and over-ripe smell all round. He held a piece of the wood under his nose. 'Smells almost like cake,' he laughed softly. 'Don't,' said the eyes of his wife, 'don't laugh. He's asleep.'

The man put the sweet over-ripe wood in the little tin stove. Then it glowed up and cast a handful of warm light through the room. The light fell bright on a tiny round face and paused for a moment. The face was only an hour old, but already it had everything that went with it: ears, nose, mouth and eyes. The eyes must be big, one could see that, although they were shut. But the mouth was open and soft breath came out of it. Nose and ears were red. 'He's alive,' thought the mother. And the little face slept.

'There are still some oat-flakes,' said the man. 'Yes,' answered the woman, 'good thing. It's cold.' The man took some more of the sweet soft wood. 'Now she's got her baby and has to freeze,' he thought. But he had no one he could hit in the face with his fists because of it. As he opened the door of the stove, another handful of light fell on the sleeping face. The woman said softly: 'Look, like a halo, do you see?' 'Halo!' he thought, and had no one he could hit in the face with his fists.

Then there were some people at the door. 'We saw the light,' they said, 'from the window. We'd like to sit down for ten minutes.' 'But we have a baby,' the man said to them. They then said nothing more, but came on into the room, blowing mist out of their noses and lifting up their feet. 'We'll be very quiet,' they whispered and lifted up their feet. Then the light fell on them.

There were three. In three old uniforms. One had a cardboard box, one a sack. And the third had no hands. 'Frostbite,' he said, and held up the stumps. Then he turned his greatcoat-pocket towards the man. There was tobacco in it and thin paper. They rolled cigarettes. But the woman said: 'No, the child.'

Then the four of them went out of the door and their cigarettes were four specks in the night. One had fat bandaged feet. He took a piece of wood out of his sack. 'A donkey,' he said, 'it took me seven months to carve it. For the baby.' He said that and gave it to the man. 'What's the matter with your feet?' asked the man. 'Water,' said the donkey-carver, 'from hunger'. 'And the other, the third man?' asked the man, as he felt the donkey in the darkness. The third man trembled in his uniform: 'Oh, nothing,' he whispered, 'it's only nerves. One just had too much fear.' Then they stubbed out their cigarettes and went in again.

They lifted up their feet and looked at the little sleeping face. The trembling one took two yellow sweets from his cardboard box and said: 'These are for your wife.'

The woman opened wide her pale blue eyes as she saw the three dark men bowed over the child. She was frightened. But then the child pushed his legs against her breast and yelled so heartily that the three dark men lifted up their feet and crept to the door. Here they nodded again, then climbed out into the night. The man watched them go. 'Peculiar Wise Men,' he said to his wife. Then he shut the door. 'Fine Wise Men they are,' he grumbled, and looked for the oat-flakes. But he had no face for his fists.

'But the baby yelled,' said the woman, 'he yelled quite loud. So they went. Just look how lively he is,' she said proudly. The face opened its mouth and yelled.

'Is he crying?' asked the man.

'No, I think he's laughing,' answered the woman.

'Almost like cake,' said the man and sniffed at the wood, 'like cake. Quite sweet.'

'Today *is* Christmas, too,' said the woman.

'Yes, Christmas,' he growled and out of the stove a handful of light fell bright on the little sleeping face.

Wolfgang Borchert

BRIGHTEST AND BEST

Brightest and best of the sons of the morning,
  Dawn on our darkness and lend us thine aid;
Star of the east, the horizon adorning,
  Guide where our infant Redeemer is laid.

Cold on His cradle the dew-drops are shining;
  Low lies His head with the beasts of the stall;
Angels adore Him in slumber reclining,
  Maker, and Monarch, and Saviour of all.

Say, shall we yield Him, in costly devotion,
  Odours of Edom and offerings divine,
Gems of the mountain and pearls of the ocean,
  Myrrh from the forest or gold from the mine?

Vainly we offer each ample oblation,
  Vainly with gifts would His favour secure;
Richer by far is the heart's adoration,
  Dearer to God are the prayers of the poor.

Brightest and best of the sons of the morning,
  Dawn on our darkness, and lend us thine aid;
Star of the east, the horizon adorning,
  Guide where our infant Redeemer is laid.

Reginald Heber

Aftermath

ST STEPHEN AND KING HEROD

Saint Stephen was a clerk
   In King Herod's hall,
And served him with bread and cloth
   As every king befall.

Stephen out of kitchen came
   With boar's head on hand
He saw a star was fair and bright
   Over Bethlehem stand.

He cast adown the boar's head
   And went into the hall;
'I forsake thee, Herod.
   And thy works all.

'I forsake thee, King Herod,
   And thy works all,
There is a child in Bethlehem born
   Is better than we all.'

'What aileth thee, Stephen?
   What is thee befall?
Lacketh thee either meat or drink
   In King Herod's hall?'

'Lacketh me neither meat nor drink
   In King Herod's hall;
There is a child in Bethlehem born
   Is better than we all.'

'What aileth thee, Stephen?
  Art mad or hast grown wroth?
Lacked thee either gold or fee
  Or any rich cloth?'

'Lacketh me neither gold nor fee
  Nor cloth nor things of greed.
There is a child in Bethlehem born
  Shall help us in our need.'

'That is all so true, Stephen,
  All so true, I know,
As if the capon in this dish
  Should come to life and crow.'

That word was not so soon said,
  That word in that hall,
The capon crew *Christus natus est*
  Among the lords all.

'Rise up, my true tormentors,
  By two and all by one,
Lead Stephen here out of this town
  And stone him with stone.'

They took Stephen
  And stoned him on the way.
And therefore is his even
  On Christ's own day.

An early English ballad

THE COMING OF THE KING

Yet if His Majesty, our sovereign lord,
Should of his own accord
Friendly himself invite,
And say, 'I'll be your guest tomorrow night,'
How should we stir ourselves, call and command
All hands to work! 'Let no man idle stand!

'Set me fine Spanish tables in the hall;
See they be fitted all;
Let there be room to eat
And order taken that there want no meat.
See every sconce and candlestick made bright,
That without tapers they may give a light.

'Look to the presence. Are the carpets spread?
The dais o'er the head?
The cushions in the chairs,
And all the candles lighted on the stairs?
Perfume the chambers, and in any case
Let each man give attendance in his place!'

Thus, if a king were coming, would we do;
And 'twere good reason, too.
For 'tis a duteous thing
To show all honour to an earthly king,
And after all our travail and our cost
So he be pleased, to think no labour lost.

But, at the coming of the King of Heaven,
All's set at six and seven;
We wallow in our sin.
Christ cannot find a chamber in the inn.
We entertain Him always like a stranger,
And, as at first, still lodge Him in the manger.

An old song

INNOCENTS' SONG

Who's that knocking on the window,
Who's that standing at the door,
What are all those presents
Lying on the kitchen floor?

Who is the smiling stranger
With hair as white as gin,
What is he doing with the children
And who could have let him in?

Why has he rubies on his fingers,
A cold, cold crown on his head,
Why, when he caws his carol,
Does the salty snow run red?

Why does he ferry my fireside
As a spider on a thread
His fingers made of fuses
And his tongue of gingerbread?

Why does the world before him
Melt in a million suns?
Why do his yellow, yearning eyes
Burn like saffron buns?

Watch where he comes walking
Out of the Christmas Flame,
Dancing, double talking:

Herod is his name.

Charles Causley

In 'Innocents' Song' the mysterious stranger becomes first Father Christmas, secondly King Herod, and thirdly a symbol of the atom bomb.

STANDING AT THE DOOR

(ARRIVING)

Where in the world has Jesus gone?
Adeste Fideles.
Where in the world has Jesus gone?
Adeste Fideles.
Where in the world has Jesus gone?
Who knows the right road from the wrong?
Adeste! Adeste Fideles!

(STANDING BEFORE)

King Jesus was born poor and gay.
Adeste Fideles.
King Jesus was born poor and gay.
Adeste Fideles.
King Jesus was born poor and gay.
Balthazar, Caspar, Melchiay,
We sing these words along your way,
King Jesus was born poor and gay!
Adeste! Adeste Fideles!

Who has the right to call Him king?
Adeste Fideles.
Who has the right to call Him king?
Adeste Fideles.
Who has the right to call Him king?
And who triumphantly shall bring
His ways and ours for gathering,
And lead us all a-Christmasing?
Adeste! Adeste Fideles!

(LEAVETAKING)

Where in the world has Jesus gone?
          Adeste Fideles.
Where in the world has Jesus gone?
          Adeste Fideles.
Who has the right to call Him king?
And who triumphantly shall bring
  His way and ours for gathering?
          Adeste Fideles!
          Adeste Fideles!
          Adeste Fideles!

Christopher Logue

Epilogue

CAROL

(To the tune of
'Once in Royal David's City')

Once an atom said to Mary
  God is weary of Mankind
Who has bulldozed all Creation
  With the iron of his mind.
    Heaven's absence cannot mend him.
    So we stand arrayed to end him.

Mary wept, remembering Jesus
  And the hour that he was slain.
Still in each man's face she looked at
  She could see the cross of pain:
    'Surely man is worth God's keeping
    While there lives but one man weeping.

'Mental pride, that halved the angels,
  Plunges man through night, alone,
While the fires of his falling
  Burn his children to the bone.
    Tell to God again how man
    Pays in men the price of man.'

So the atom flew to Heaven
  And in stillness Heaven heard
What a solitary confinement
  Is man's deafness to the Word:
    What an agony of thinking,
    In what death-cell silence sinking.

Then God touched the little atom
   And the altered heavens cried:
'What was Danger shall be Beauty
And the atom be man's bride;
     And the frailty of her defenses
     Bring man's iron to its senses.'

Ted Hughes

GOOD WILL TO MEN

One word ere yet the evening ends,
  Let's close it with a parting rhyme,
And pledge a hand to all our friends,
  As fits the merry Christmas time. . . .
As fits the solemn Christmas tide,
  As fits the holy Christmas birth,
Be this, good friends, our carol still—
Be peace on earth, be peace on earth,
  To men of gentle will.

W. M. Thackeray

THE KING IS FOUND

Let your bearing towards one another arise out of your life in Christ Jesus. For the divine nature was his from the first; yet he did not think to snatch at equality with God, but made himself nothing, assuming the nature of a slave. Bearing the human likeness, revealed in human shape, he humbled himself, and in obedience accepted even death—death on a cross. Therefore God raised him to the heights and bestowed on him the name above all names, that at the name of Jesus every knee should bow—in heaven, on earth, and in the depths—and every tongue confess, 'Jesus Christ is Lord', to the glory of God the Father.

St Paul to the Philippians

SOURCES AND ACKNOWLEDGEMENTS

Prophecy

PREPARE YE THE WAY OF THE LORD Isaiah 40.1–11; from the Authorized Version of the Bible.

THE WORD TO BE MADE FLESH John 1.6–14; from the New English Bible.

A MOMENT IN TIME T. S. Eliot (1888–1965); extracts from Choruses from "The Rock" '; reprinted by permission of Faber and Faber Ltd from *Collected Poems 1909–1962* by T. S. Eliot.

THE ANNUNCIATION Luke 1.26–38; from the New English Bible.

THE CHERRY-TREE CAROL An early ballad of unknown date and authorship, perhaps one of the oldest known ballads in English before *c.*1380.

AS JOSEPH WAS A-WALKIN' An early ballad, sometimes recognized as Part 2 of 'The cherry-tree carol'.

A Winter Birth

IN THE BLEAK MID-WINTER Christina Georgina Rossetti (1830–94); 'A Christmas Carol' from *Poems of Christina Rossetti*, chosen and edited by William M. Rossetti, Macmillan 1904.

A CHRISTMAS CAROL Christina Georgina Rossetti; from G. H. Holroyd, *The Christmas Dramatic Book*, Macmillan 1956.

NEW PRINCE, NEW POMP Robert Southwell (1561?–95).

A CHRISTMAS CAROL Laurence Housman (1865–1959); from *The Collected Poems of Laurence Housman*, Sidgwick and Jackson 1937; by permission of the Executors of the Laurence Housman Estate and Jonathan Cape Ltd.

A COUNTRY CAROL Philip Oakes (1928–); from *In the Affirmative*, André Deutsch 1968.

THE SHEEP ON BLACKENING FIELDS Charles Causley (1917–); from *Collected Poems 1951–1975*, Macmillan 1975.

SONG FOR A WINTER BIRTH Vernon Scannell (1922–); from *The Winter Man,* Allison and Busby 1971.

The Shepherds

THE BIRTH AND ITS TELLING TO THE SHEPHERDS Luke 2.1–20; from the New English Bible.

SHEPHERD'S SONG Author unknown.

THE SHEPHERDS' CAROL Author unknown.

Mother and Child

A CRADLE HYMN Isaac Watts (1647–1748); from G. H. Holroyd, *The Christmas Dramatic Book,* Macmillan 1956.

A CHRISTMAS CAROL G. K. Chesterton (1847–1936); from *The Wild Knight and Other Poems,* Dent 1935; by permission of Miss Dorothy Collins and J. M. Dent and Sons Ltd.

MOTHER AND MAIDEN Author unknown (fifteenth century).

A ROCKING HYMN George Wither (1588–1667).

Carol Singers

CAROL SINGERS Thomas Hardy (1840–1928); from *Under the Greenwood Tree,* Macmillan 1872; by permission of the Trustees of the Hardy Estate and Macmillan, London and Basingstoke.

A Child's Christmas

THROUGH A CHILD'S EYES Vera Brittain (1893–1970); from *Testament of Friendship,* Macmillan 1940; by permission of the author's literary executors, Sir George Catlin and Paul Berry.

A VILLAGE CHRISTMAS IN BOHEMIA Adalbert Stifter (1805–1868); from *Rock Crystal,* Bantam Books, a translation by Harry Steinhauer of *Bergkristall* by Adalbert Stifter, first published in 1845 under the title *Der Heiliger Abend* (Christmas Eve). It was later rewritten under its present title because the glass-like clarity of rock crystal is a fitting symbol of the spirit that pervades the tale. Reprinted by permission of the translator.

A CHILD'S CHRISTMAS PRAYER Mary Farrah; from the *United Methodist Sunday School Hymnal.*

Christmas Tree

TO A YOUNG WRETCH Robert Frost (1874–1963); from *The Poetry of Robert Frost,* edited by Edward Connery Latham, Jonathan Cape 1971; by permission of the Estate of Robert Frost, the editor, and publishers. (Canadian publishers: Holt, Rinehart & Winston, Inc.)

THE CULTIVATION OF CHRISTMAS TREES T. S. Eliot (1888–1965); reprinted by permission of Faber and Faber Ltd from *Collected Poems 1909–1962* by T. S. Eliot.

Christmas Eve

CHRISTMAS EVE IN PETROGRAD Hugh Walpole (1884–1941); from *The Secret City,* Macmillan 1919; by permission of Sir Rupert Hart-Davis.

CHRISTMAS EVE AT SEA John Masefield (1878–1967); from *The Collected Poems of John Masefield,* Copyright 1916 by John Masefield, renewed 1944. Heinemann 1923; by permission of the Society of Authors, as the literary representative of the Estate of John Masefield, and Macmillan Publishing Co., Inc.

CHRISTMAS EVE AT DINGLEY DELL Charles Dickens (1812–70); from *Pickwick Papers* (1837).

Christmas Day

ON THE MORNING OF CHRIST'S NATIVITY John Milton (1608–74); the opening stanza of Milton's ode *On the Morning of Christ's Nativity* (1629).

THE BURNING BABE Robert Southwell (1561?–95).

PERILOUS TIMES John Evelyn (1620–1706); from the *Diary of John Evelyn* (1818).

MR PEPYS'S CHRISTMAS DAY Samuel Pepys (1633–1703); from the *Diary of Samuel Pepys* (1825).

AT SEA, 1675 Henry Teonge (1621–90); from the *Diary of the Rev. Henry Teonge.*

CHRISTMAS DAY, 1784 Henry White; from the *Diary of the Rev. Henry White.*

ON CHRISTMAS DAY Thomas Traherne (1637?–74). (Extracts only).

THIS DAY Sir Frederick Still (1868–1941); from *Childhood*, John Murray 1941.

Celebration

A PSALM FOR CHRISTMAS DAY MORNING Thomas Pestel (1585–1667).

RING THE BELLS, THE CHRISTMAS BELLS Agnes Burney; from the *United Methodist Sunday School Hymnal*.

HEAP ON MORE WOOD Sir Walter Scott (1771–1832); extract from *Marmion* (1808).

MERRY PIPING TIME OF CHRISTMAS Charles Lamb (1775–1834); from *Sketches and Essays*.

SIR ROGER DE COVERLEY Joseph Addison (1672–1719); from *The Spectator*.

THE SQUIRE'S CHRISTMAS BANQUET Washington Irving (1783–1859); from *The Sketch-Book* (1820).

AN ODE ON THE BIRTH OF OUR SAVIOUR Robert Herrick (1591–1674).

THE SHEPHERD AND THE KING Author unknown.

THE CRATCHITS' CHRISTMAS DINNER Charles Dickens (1812–70); from *A Christmas Carol* (1843).

THE VICTORIAN CHRISTMAS PANTOMIME Charles Dickens, writing to Miss Mary Boyle, 28 December 1860; from *The Dickens Theatrical Reader*, edited by Edgar and Eleanor Johnson, Gollancz 1964.

PRESENT MIRTH AND PAST AFFECTION Mazo de la Roche (1885–1961); from *Jalna*, Macmillan 1927; by permission of the publisher.

CHRISTMAS MINIATURE Herbert Palmer (1880–1961); privately published 1928.

The Promise of Christmas

THAT HOLY THING George MacDonald (1824–1905).

CRADLED IN A MANGER G. Stringer Rowe (1830–1913); from the *United Methodist Sunday School Hymnal*.

THE HOUSE OF CHRISTMAS G. K. Chesterton (1874–1936); from *The Collected Poems of G. K. Chesterton*, Burns, Oates and Washbourne 1927; by permission of Miss Dorothy Collins.

THE OXEN Thomas Hardy (1840–1928); from *The Complete Poems* (New Wessex Edition) by Thomas Hardy, Macmillan 1976; by permission of the Trustees of the Hardy Estate and the publisher.

YULE-TIDE FIRES Author unknown.

CHRISTMAS John Betjeman (1906–); from *Collected Poems*, John Murray 1958.

DIVINE CHARITY: DIVINE ART A. E. Whitham (1879–1938); from *The Discipline and Culture of the Spiritual Life*, Hodder & Stoughton 1938.

The Kings

THE WISE WISE-MEN Matthew 2.1–12; from the Authorized Version of the Bible.

JOURNEY OF THE MAGI T. S. Eliot (1888–1965); reprinted by permission of Faber and Faber Ltd from *Collected Poems 1909–1962* by T. S. Eliot.

KINGS CAME RIDING Charles Williams (1886–1945); from *Modern Verse for Little Children*, chosen by Michael Williams (1927); reprinted by permission of Oxford University Press.

THE THREE DARK MAGI Wolfgang Borchert (1921–47); from *The Man Outside*, a translation by David Porter (Calder and Boyars 1966) of *Die drei dunklen Könige* by Wolfgang Borchert, published by Rowohlt Verlag 1946.

BRIGHTEST AND BEST Reginald Heber (1783–1826).

Aftermath

ST STEPHEN AND KING HEROD An early English ballad, author and date unknown.

THE COMING OF THE KING It is believed that these verses were once part of a longer poem, and some scholars have attributed them to Henry Vaughan; but, though they bear his inflection and though the Christ Church manuscript (in which they were discovered) contains other stanzas by Vaughan, it is impossible to say definitely that they are his.

INNOCENTS' SONG Charles Causley (1917–); from *Collected Poems 1951–1975*, Macmillan 1975.

STANDING AT THE DOOR Christopher Logue (1926–); copyright © 1965 by Christopher Logue.

Epilogue

CAROL Ted Hughes (1930–); copyright © 1965 by Ted Hughes.

GOOD WILL TO MEN W. M. Thackeray (1811–63).

THE KING IS FOUND St Paul to the Philippians 2.5–11; from the New English Bible.

Thanks for permission to reproduce copyright material are extended to the authors, publishers, and other copyright-holders included in the above list.

INDEX OF AUTHORS